P9-DWD-529

JOJO
the

JANE BARCLAY

ILLUSTRATED BY
ESPERANÇA MELO

TUNDRA BOOKS

Published in Canada by Tundra Books,
75 Sherbourne Street, Toronto, Ontario M5A 2P9

Published in the United States by Tundra Books of Northern New York,
P.O. Box 1030, Plattsburgh, New York 12901

Library of Congress Control Number: 2011923468

Library and Archives Canada Cataloguing in Publication

Barclay, Jane, 1957-
JoJo the giant / by Jane Barclay ; illustrated by Esperança Melo.

ISBN 978-0-88776-976-4

I. Melo, Esperança II. Title.

PS8553.A74327J6 2012 jC813.'54 C2011-901449-1

We acknowledge the financial support of the Government of Canada through the Book Publishing Industry Development Program (BPIDP) and that of the Government of Ontario through the Ontario Media Development Corporation's Ontario Book Initiative. We further acknowledge the support of the Canada Council for the Arts and the Ontario Arts Council for our publishing program.

ONTARIO ARTS COUNCIL
CONSEIL DES ARTS DE L'ONTARIO

Printed and bound in China

1 2 3 4 5 6 17 16 15 14 13 12

To hard-working moms and those who appreciate them.
– J. B.

In memory of my father, Fernando Feliciano de Melo,
who was passionate about books and whose engaging personality
and poetic spirit looms large in my life.
– E. M.

DELI

JoJo was a very small boy with big dreams. He lived with his mother and a marmalade cat in an apartment over a deli. His mother was a mail carrier, and rain or shine, she delivered packages and letters. Every afternoon she picked him up after school, and they would walk home together.

Inside, his mother would sit on the couch, rubbing her tired feet while JoJo poured the tea. Then he'd wait until she had at least three sips before he asked the big question.

"How much did I grow today?"

His mother would look him up and down while JoJo held his breath.

"This much," she'd say.

JoJo would sigh, staring at the space between her finger and her thumb that was no wider than a hair.

“Trust me, JoJo. Good things come in small packages,” his mother would say.

But JoJo wasn’t so sure. The way he saw it, bigger was better. So, he ate all of his broccoli. He drank all of his milk. And when no one was looking, he stood on his tiptoes and imagined he was a tree; a skyscraper; a giraffe.

OES THAT
S WORLD!

One Saturday, JoJo's mother asked him to run to the store for some milk. He sped down the street and stopped at Smiling Sam's Shoe Shop where he noticed a poster in the window. It was an advertisement for a race sponsored by "Rocket Racers: The Running Shoes That Are Out Of This World!" The race was to be held in a week, and first prize was a pair of red Rocket Racers – the ones with silver stars on the sides.

A spotlight shone on the pair in the window, and JoJo stared at them in awe. He thought of his mother and how hard she worked. He wiggled his toes in his sneakers and remembered the sad look on her face when she had to tell him that something was too expensive. He opened the shop door and stepped inside.

A tall boy with slicked-back hair and gleaming white teeth grinned at JoJo.

"Is this where you sign up for the race?" JoJo asked.

"You must be signing up for your big brother," the boy snorted.

"Actually, I'm signing up for me."

"Well, good luck, squirt. Big Tony's my name, and speed is my game!" He gave JoJo a pat on the head and sauntered outside.

ROCKETRACERS
THE RUNNING SHOES THAT
ARE OUT OF THIS WORLD!

JoJo added his name to the sheet and dashed off to the milk store. "Yo! Yo!" shouted the bullies on the corner as he zoomed past. "Check out the runaway shrimp!"

JoJo did what he always did when the bullies were around. He ran even faster.

That night, after she tucked him in, JoJo told his mother about the red Rocket Racers.

"But JoJo, why do you want these shoes so badly? I've had the same pair of shoes for years, and they're perfectly fine."

JoJo glanced at her plain brown shoes with the well-worn heels and pretended to yawn. After she kissed him goodnight and closed the door, JoJo climbed out of bed and stared at himself in the mirror.

"Good things come in small packages," he said in a big voice.

The boy in the mirror didn't look so sure.

On race day, JoJo and his mother arrived at the track. Big Tony was hamming it up for some reporters, while Smiling Sam stood with a pair of red Rocket Racers and posed for the photographers.

“Clear the track, clear the track!” said the announcer over the loudspeaker.

JoJo stood behind the start line with trembling legs. The track official raised his starter’s pistol.

“Runners take your marks . . .”

JoJo crouched in the ready position. Out of the corner of his eye, he could see Big Tony flexing his muscles. JoJo gulped.

“Get set . . .”

The runners froze, eyes focused on the track ahead.

BANG!

Off they flew along the course in a blur of arms and legs. Around the bend the runners charged, with Big Tony in the lead. JoJo was right on his heels. Down the final stretch they ran. It was going to be a close race and the crowd rose to its feet.

JoJo ran as fast as he could, but Big Tony with his long legs, was a stride ahead. They were closing in on the finish line when a chant rose from somewhere in the crowd.

"Go shrimp, go! Go shrimp, go!"

It was the bullies in the bleachers.

Big Tony heard them, looked around, and grinned at JoJo.

"Hey, shrimp! I'll wait for you at the finish line," he yelled.

Not if I get there first, thought JoJo.

Then he did what he always did when the bullies were around. He ran even faster. With a burst of broccoli-fueled speed, he zipped past an astonished Big Tony and across the finish line. The crowd went wild.

That night after ice-cream sundaes, JoJo lay in bed with his trophy on one side of him and his mother on the other.

"How much did I grow today?" he asked.

His mother smiled. On her feet was the pair of red Rocket Racers, the ones with the silver stars on the sides.

"This much!" his mother said. She opened her arms as wide as they could go and gave him a gigantic hug.

After she kissed him and closed the door, JoJo climbed out of bed and looked at himself in the mirror. He imagined he was a cheetah; a bobsled; a rocket.

The boy who smiled back was ten feet tall.